First-Grade Bunny

For Reza, who's not scared
of anything at all.
—M. M.

ALADDIN PAPERBACKS
An imprint of Simon & Schuster Children's Publishing Division
1230 Avenue of the Americas, New York, NY 10020
Text copyright © 2005 by Simon & Schuster, Inc.
Illustrations copyright © 2005 by Mike Gordon
All rights reserved, including the right of reproduction
in whole or in part in any form.
ALADDIN PAPERBACKS, READY-TO-READ,
and colophon are trademarks of Simon & Schuster, Inc.
Also available in an Aladdin library edition.
Designed by Sammy Yuen Jr.
The text of this book was set in CentSchbook BT.
Manufactured in the United States of America
First Aladdin Paperbacks edition February 2005
4 6 8 10 9 7 5 3
Library of Congress Cataloging-in-Publication Data
McNamara, Margaret.
First-grade bunny / Margaret McNamara ; illustrated by Mike Gordon.
p. cm.—(Robin Hill School) (Ready-to-read)
Summary: Everyone in Mrs. Connor's first-grade class loves their visitor,
Sparky the bunny, except Reza, who tries to overcome his fear when the
teacher gives him a special job.
ISBN 0-689-86427-2 (pbk.)—ISBN 0-689-86428-0 (lib. bdg.)
[1. Rabbits as pets—Fiction. 2. Fear—Fiction. 3. Schools—Fiction.]
I. Gordon, Mike, ill. II. Title. III. Series.
PZ7.M232518Fi 2005 [E]—dc22 2004008889

Robin Hill School

First-Grade Bunny

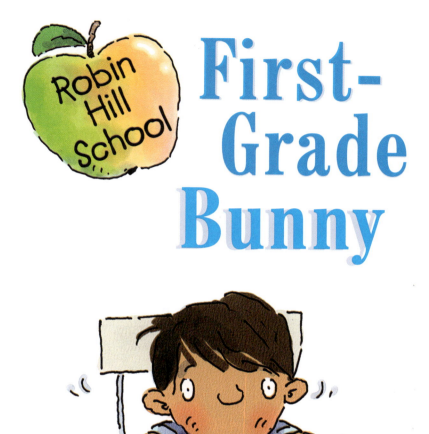

Written by Margaret McNamara
Illustrated by Mike Gordon

Ready-to-Read
Aladdin Paperbacks
New York   London   Toronto   Sydney

"We have a visitor,"
Mrs. Connor said.
"A bunny rabbit!"

"Yay!" Katie said.

"Oh," Reza said.

Reza was not afraid
of much.

But he was afraid
of bunnies.

"This is Sparky,"
said Mrs. Connor.
"You will all get a turn
to take care of her."

"Me first," said Michael.

"Me second," said Mia.

"Me last," said Reza.

The next day,
Becky and Emma
fed Sparky
baby carrots.

The day after,
Nick changed
Sparky's water.

Michael and Ayanna
cleaned Sparky's cage.

Mrs. Connor helped.

The day after that,
Hannah told the class
how to pet Sparky.

"Ask first," she said.
"And be gentle."

Mrs. Connor saw Reza
in the corner.

"Tomorrow, you will
take care of Sparky,"
she said.

That night,
Reza had a scary dream.

In his dream

there was a big, big bunny.

The bunny was chasing Reza.

And Reza was wearing only
his underpants.

At school the next morning
Reza looked at Sparky.
Sparky was panting.

Reza did not want to show
that he was afraid
of a bunny.

"I have a good job
for you,"
said Mrs. Connor.

"Please draw
a picture of Sparky."
Reza took out
his crayons.

He drew his best picture.

"I think I will be ready
to pet a bunny
someday soon," said Reza.

"I think you will too,"
said Mrs. Connor.